HOT TRAIL TO DANGER

Nikki shook her head and bolted blindly through the brush. A mixture of fear and uncertainty flooded over her. One thought kept running through her mind: Find the children and make it back to the canoe before the fire cut her off.

She started shouting. "Hey! Are you there? Can you hear me?"

The smoke was a thick black cloud sweeping toward her just ahead of the raging fire. An orange tint settled in the tops of the trees. Nikki tried not to look at it.

She would face the fire soon enough.

"Please, please let me find them," Nikki prayed. She cupped her hands and yelled as loud as her voice could carry, "Where are you? I'm here to help. You have to answer me."

After a few more yards Nikki stopped. She had gone as far as the shore would allow. There was a sheer drop of a hundred feet in front of her. Though she had never been down this fork, she knew exactly where she was.

Deadman's Drop.

GARY PAULSEN
WORLD OF ADVENTURE

ESCAPE FROM
FIRE MOUNTAIN

A YEARLING BOOK

Published by
Bantam Doubleday Dell Books for Young Readers
a division of
Bantam Doubleday Dell Publishing Group, Inc.
1540 Broadway
New York, New York 10036

ISBN: 0-440-41025-8

Series design: Barbara Berger

Interior illustration by Michael David Biegel

Printed in the United States of America

February 1995

10   9   8   7   6   5   4   3   2   1

OPM

Dear Readers:

Real adventure is many things—it's danger and daring and sometimes even a struggle for life or death. From competing in the Iditarod dogsled race across Alaska to sailing the Pacific Ocean, I've experienced some of this adventure myself. I try to capture this spirit in my stories, and each time I sit down to write, that challenge is a bit of an adventure in itself.

You're all a part of this adventure as well. Over the years I've had the privilege of talking with many of you in schools, and this book is the result of hearing firsthand what you want to read about most—power-packed action and excitement.

You asked for it—so hang on tight while we jump into another thrilling story in my World of Adventure.

Gary Paulsen

ESCAPE FROM FIRE MOUNTAIN

CHAPTER 1

Nikki Roberts's green eyes flew open. The morning sun was pouring through her bedroom window. She grabbed the alarm clock and frowned. It was Monday and already after seven o'clock. "Traitor. Of all the mornings for you to fall down on your job . . ."

A door slammed downstairs.

The tall blond girl let the clock fall on the bed and frantically pulled on her jeans.

A voice carried from below. "Hurry up, Nikki. We're almost ready." It was her dad, and his voice held a note of impatience.

Jim Roberts was a well-respected outfitter and guide in the Wabash Mountains. The family-operated Tall Pines Hunting Lodge functioned as a headquarters for his guided elk hunts. It catered to people from all over the country and was always full in the winter, with a long waiting list.

Now it was off-season. No hunting could take place in the summer, so there were no visitors. Nikki's parents were going to the city, several hundred miles away, for a week to help her uncle Joe, who was recovering from knee surgery.

Nikki had convinced her folks that she was old enough to stay behind and take care of things. After all, she had been raised up here, and at thirteen she was mature enough to remember to feed the stock and keep an eye on the place.

She took the wooden stairs two at a time and found her mom in the kitchen checking for the tenth time a list of things for Nikki to do.

Nikki peered at the list over her mother's

shoulder. "Don't worry, Mom. Everything will be fine. You'll only be gone a few days."

Her mom put the list back on the refrigerator. "I know. But if there *is* a problem, you'll get on the phone and call for help, right? The CB base radio doesn't have the range to get out beyond the mountains."

"She knows all that." Nikki's dad winked at her over the top of her mother's head. He picked up the last suitcase. "You've been over it with her at least a dozen times. Now come on. We told Joe we'd be there before nightfall."

Nikki walked them out to the pickup. Her mom looked around anxiously at the woodland that surrounded the lodge. The river, peaceful and reassuring, tumbled playfully under the log bridge a few yards in front of them. She sighed, hugged her daughter, and got in on the passenger side. "I put Uncle Joe's number right beside the phone."

"I know, Mom. And on the microwave, the TV, and the bathroom mirror. I won't lose it, promise."

Nikki's dad put his arm around her. "Stay close to home, kiddo. No long horseback rides or canoe trips, okay?"

"Dad, you're as bad as Mom."

"Can I help it if I want my head wrangler and chief cook in one piece when I get back?"

"What could go wrong? All I have to do is feed the horses, take reservations, and lie around and eat popcorn."

Her dad stepped into the truck and laughed. "Well, at least go easy on the popcorn." He started the engine. "We should be back by Sunday."

"Good-bye, Nikki." Her mother waved. The truck rumbled down the dirt drive, and they were gone.

Nikki watched them cross over the bridge and disappear down into the valley. A funny feeling of excitement came over her. She picked up a rock and threw it as far out into the river as she could. It skimmed easily across the glimmering surface. Nikki smiled. Then she turned and raced back to the house to begin her first day of independence.

CHAPTER 2

The horses were fed, and there was nothing worth watching on television. Nikki had straightened the entire house, and it was still before noon.

She pulled on her riding boots and wandered back out to the barn. Goblin, her favorite horse, put his head over the corral fence, and Nikki stroked his sleek black neck.

"Dad didn't say I couldn't go riding, you know. He just said not to take long rides." Nikki patted him between the ears. "Anyway, what's long to some people is really not very long to others. Have you ever noticed that, Goblin?"

The horse blinked his big dark eyes at her. She ruffled his ears. "I'm glad you're so agreeable."

Nikki brushed his smooth coat, slid on his bridle, and lightly tossed a blanket on his broad back. She grabbed her saddle, moved to Goblin's left side, and swung it up. When everything was in place, she pulled the cinch tight and stepped up.

In minutes she was heading up the north trail toward Sugar Loaf Ridge. There were some dark clouds in the distance, but it would take a few hours for them to get here. In the meantime, she would take a leisurely ride and check on the elk herd. Then she would come back, make an embarrassing amount of popcorn, and pig out while she watched movies on TV.

Nikki wound her way up the narrow trail, working Goblin into an easy canter. Giant pines lined the trail on both sides. Every so often a rabbit would dart out of the brush and race alongside Goblin, then disappear back into the undergrowth. Goblin whinnied playfully each time. He seemed to enjoy the game.

Several miles up Nikki topped out on a small peak overlooking a grassy meadow. To her right were beautiful snowcapped mountains. It was peaceful here. She stopped and took a deep breath of the fresh air.

In the meadow below a movement caught her eye, and she slid the binoculars from the saddlebags.

Bighorns.

A large band of bighorn sheep was passing through from the salt licks on its way up to the high mountains. The big rams marched like royalty with their curled horns held high. The spring lambs jumped over their mothers, chased one another, and butted heads with an unending supply of energy.

Staying in the shadows of the tall trees, Nikki urged Goblin forward until he was right at the edge of the meadow. Silently she stepped off her horse and tied him loosely to a branch. She slowly crawled closer, using the tall grass for cover.

The lambs were still romping about. One of

the mothers got tired of being hurdled and butted a little one end over end. The tiny lamb tumbled to the ground in a woolly heap. Nikki nearly laughed out loud.

From nowhere a rifle shot cracked the morning and echoed through the valley.

The band of sheep scattered, but it was too late. A large ram fell to the ground.

Nikki froze.

Poachers.

Through the tall grass she watched two camouflage-colored four-wheelers drive up to the ram. Two rough-looking men jumped off and went mechanically to work, slicing and hacking at the throat of the dead animal. They were after its head. Within minutes it was severed. Carefully the poachers wrapped the beautiful curled horns and tied the ram's head on the back of one of the four-wheelers.

Nikki held her breath. No telling what they would do if they found her there as a witness.

One of the men suddenly looked in her direction. He had cold blue eyes and a pointed red beard. She tried to sink lower into the grass. The man began walking right at her. He passed so close he almost stepped on her hand.

A horse whinnied. It was Goblin. He had somehow gotten loose and decided to join Nikki in the meadow.

The man with the red beard grabbed the horse's reins. "Someone's out here, Frank. They probably saw the whole thing."

The man called Frank finished tying the ram's head and wiped the blood off his hands. "Quit worrying. It's just a loose horse. You've been jumpy all day."

The bearded man scowled. "I'll quit worrying when we close down this operation. We've got too much at stake to get caught."

"We're not going to get caught. No one lives in these mountains. There's one old hunting lodge and no people around for miles."

"Then where did he come from?" Red Beard looked at the horse.

"Like I said, he got loose. Probably threw a greenhorn somewhere down in the valley. Give him a swat and send him on his way. We've got more important things to worry about."

The bearded man tied the horse's reins to-gether and hit him hard on the rear. Goblin jumped forward and raced through the trees.

"Don't just stand there," Frank snarled. "Let's get this one back to camp and measure the horns. If it's as big as I think it is, we'll only need three more to fill our order."

The two men climbed on the four-wheelers and drove away, leaving the animal's carcass lying in the grass.

Nikki waited until she could no longer hear their engines before she stood up. Her shoul-ders slumped. Goblin was nowhere in sight, and it was a good four miles back to the lodge.

Thunder rolled from the east, and lightning crashed behind it. The dark clouds had moved in while the poachers had kept her captive in the grass. Dime-size raindrops started falling.

Nikki shivered, pulled up her shirt collar, and ran.

CHAPTER 3

 Goblin was waiting patiently by the barn when Nikki got home. By the time she unsaddled him and made it to the house she was thoroughly drenched. Water ran off her hair and clothes and made puddles on the floor.

The lightning was worse now, striking every few minutes. Nikki looked out the narrow window next to the front door. Another flash popped near the barn, and the ground turned a ghostly white.

Nikki leaned against the wall to catch her breath, wondering what to do about the poachers. "The sheriff," she whispered out loud. Leaving a wet trail, she headed for the kitchen and picked up the phone.

It was dead.

"Oh great." Nikki brushed a piece of long blond hair out of her eyes. She snapped her fingers. "The CB." It didn't have great range, but it would be worth a try.

She ran to her dad's office and had just turned the doorknob when she heard the radio squelch. A garbled voice crackled through the static.

". . . please anybody . . . fire . . . need help, over." It was a child's voice, a boy's, but it shook with fear or pain. "Can you . . . me . . . near the bend in the river. Help us . . . over."

Nikki stayed off the radio, waiting to hear a response, not wanting to interfere with an emergency. There was no answer.

". . . lost . . . fire coming closer . . . anybody hear . . ."

Still no response.

Nikki picked up the handset. *I'll wait a sec-*

ond longer, she thought. *Maybe someone will call him.*

"We . . . help . . . sister's hurt . . . please . . ." The voice was torn by static.

Nikki listened intently, but there were no other transmissions. There would be no help for them.

"I can help you. I'll get you out." Nikki found herself yelling into the microphone. "Can you hear me?"

Except for the buzz of static, the radio was silent.

They hadn't received her.

Nikki tried again. "Can you hold on? Can you tell me where you are? Over."

". . . white rocks . . . can any . . . help us . . ."

The speaker suddenly went dead, as if someone had unplugged the radio.

The poachers would have to wait. Nikki raced upstairs and checked her survival bag. It was always kept packed with dried food, extra clothing, and other gear so that when her father needed her on short notice, she would be ready. She made an attempt to dry off, changed her clothes, and slipped into a raincoat.

By the time she got outside, the weather had begun to clear. The wind still whipped, but the brunt of the storm had moved on.

She started for the barn to resaddle Goblin but changed her mind.

A canoe would be faster.

The boy had described white rocks near a bend in the river. That could only be one place—Deadman's Drop.

The rapids.

Nikki ran to the boat shed and pulled a fiberglass canoe off the rack. She carried it on her shoulders to the water and then went back for paddles and a life vest.

She threw her survival pack in the middle, slid into the canoe, and pushed off.

CHAPTER 4

 As Nikki paddled down the rushing mountain river, she searched the horizon for a sign of the fire. Sure enough, a thin gray haze hung just over the top of one of the mountain ridges downriver. She thought she could smell the smoke.

Her dad had been called upon many times in the past to help fight fires in the area, and she had learned that lightning was usually the cause. She was hoping that there had been enough rainfall in that area to keep it from spreading too far.

Nikki breathed a sigh of relief when she

thought about home. The lodge had just received a good soaking. It would be safe for the time being from spot fires.

A loud noise brought her attention back to the river.

She felt it more than heard it. From just ahead came a slow, constant thundering sound.

The first white water.

She reached it in seconds. This small set of rapids wasn't considered too difficult. Nikki had run them many times with her father. Together they had traveled the north fork of the river all the way to Harrison.

Once through, she straightened her back and dropped her knees to the floor of the canoe. Readjusting her grip on the paddle, she began looking ahead for rocks.

The frothing white water tumbled and was loud enough now to block out all other sound as it crashed over the large rocks and curled under in eddies.

The speed of the canoe increased, drawn by the current. The canoe seemed to hang on the edge of a rapid for a second.

Then it shot up.

Nikki could no longer see the river in front of the canoe. Water rolled and splashed over her. The hull grated on a rock. She screamed at herself for not seeing it sooner.

Despite her best efforts to stop it, the stern of the canoe started to turn. In a matter of seconds the small craft whipped around and plunged blindly backward.

She tried to push against passing boulders to turn it back, but the current was too strong.

Then it hit hard.

The canoe scraped its hull against a huge rock and lurched to a stop. A rip could fill the craft with water almost instantly. Nikki quickly inspected it for leaks. She ran her hands over the sides and up and down the bottom, feeling for even the tiniest tear. She found none.

"Okay." Nikki used the paddle to push free from the snag and continued downstream. "Let's get it right this time."

The water in front of her was calmer for the next mile or so. Occasionally the current tugged at her, but she guided the little canoe through with no more problems.

The smoke was easier to see now. It was boiling black from just beyond the next hill.

Nikki let the canoe drift close to shore. The river forked here, and Deadman's Drop would be coming up. She could take her chances and maybe get to the kids faster by trying the dangerous rapids, or she could pull the canoe out now and go overland.

"It won't be faster if I'm dead," Nikki said out loud. She stepped out of the canoe onto the pebbly river bottom and pulled the craft up to the shore, then secured it to a tree with the bow rope.

Quickly she took off her life vest and shrugged out of the thin raincoat. Slinging the pack over her shoulder, she headed toward the smoke.

Nikki wished she had some way of knowing exactly where the boy and his sister were. Since he had mentioned the river, she decided the best thing to do was stay close to it. Maybe they would be waiting somewhere near the rapids.

It hadn't rained here. The brush along the

shore was dry and brittle. There would be nothing to slow the fire. It was free to burn in any direction it chose.

A tangled mass of clawing brush tore at her clothes. She worked through it as fast as she could, the sharp leaves drawing blood from her hands. When it got too thick, Nikki waded in the water to avoid it.

Around the next twist in the river, a wall of pale gray smoke—silhouetted in solid black—rose from the trees just a few hundred yards from her. The underside of the smoke was illuminated in an eerie reddish glow. For a moment she stood transfixed, fascinated in a way she couldn't explain.

Nikki shook her head and bolted blindly through the brush. A mixture of fear and uncertainty flooded over her. One thought ran through her mind: Find the children and make it back to the canoe before the fire cut her off.

She started shouting. "Hey! Are you there? Can you hear me?"

The smoke was a thick black cloud sweeping toward her just ahead of the raging fire. An orange tint settled in the tops of the trees. Nikki tried not to look at it.

She would face the fire soon enough.

"Please, please let me find them," Nikki prayed. She cupped her hands and yelled as loud as her voice could carry, "Where are you? I'm here to help. You have to answer me."

After a few more yards Nikki stopped. She had gone as far as the shore would allow. There was a sheer drop of a hundred feet in front of her. Though she had never been down this fork, she knew exactly where she was.

Deadman's Drop.

The roar from the rapids drowned out her shouting. The air was hot, and pieces of soot flew around her.

Think! Nikki tried desperately to concentrate. *If you were a frightened child trapped in a forest fire, what would you do?*

She stood on the edge of the cliff and watched the crashing white water below.

A tiny hand reached up and touched her shoe.

CHAPTER 5

Dropping to her knees, Nikki grabbed the hand and pulled a chubby little girl with dark brown curls and big black eyes to the top of the overhang. A boy about eight years old, with the same color eyes and lighter hair, dressed in jeans and a torn green T-shirt, climbed up behind her. He was carrying a toy walkie-talkie.

"What on earth . . ." Nikki stared.

The girl, who looked to be maybe four years old, was wearing a dirty pink jumper. Dried tears stained her cheeks. She sat in Nikki's lap and hugged her hard. "Me and James thought nobody could hear us."

"What are you two doing out here?"

The boy looked sheepish. "It was all an accident. We borrowed my grandpa's canoe, and it sorta got away from us."

"I heard parts of your message on my CB radio and came as soon as I could." Nikki looked them over. "Are you both all right?"

"Molly fell off the cliff and hurt her foot. I don't know how bad it is, but it's all red and swollen. That's how we found that ledge down there." The boy pointed below him.

Nikki peered over the edge. Jutting out from the face of the cliff was a small rock overhang. Far below it the rapids churned violently.

The wind was picking up. Nikki looked behind her. If she had been alone, she would have tried for the canoe, but if she had to carry the girl, it would be next to impossible. The fire had almost made it to the river. The flames were as tall as the trees. They arched, casting a threatening light through the dark, billowing smoke.

Nikki stepped back, gave her pack to the

22

boy, and picked up the little girl. "We've got to hurry now. James, I'm going to carry Molly on my back. You've got to stay up with me no matter what—understand?"

The boy's dirt-streaked face was serious. He nodded.

Nikki shifted Molly to her back and set out at the quickest pace she could manage and still carry her precious cargo. James stayed right on her heels.

The fire was close, too close. Nikki's eyes were blurred by smoke and sweat. The trees crackled and the wind carried red-hot splinters that singed holes in the children's clothes and stung their skin. Where they stood would soon be nothing but blackened stalks and burned earth. There was only one hope of escape.

Nikki's plan was to get as far away from the fire as possible and then try to go around it. If they managed it, they could rest somewhere for the night and head out for the lodge in the morning—that is, if the wind cooperated and didn't send the fire chasing after them.

As if it could read her thoughts, a sudden

gust of wind blew hot cinders in their direction. A deafening crack split the air and a large tree limb hit the ground in front of them.

Nikki jumped backward, but a tall orange flame licked out and caught her pants leg on fire. She dumped Molly to the side, dropped to the ground, and rolled to put it out.

Slowly Nikki sat up and examined herself. There didn't seem to be any real damage. Her leg was black but not burned and her jeans and sock were only singed.

Molly looked like she was about ready to start crying again. Nikki scooped her up and motioned for James, who was staring wide-eyed, to follow.

"We'll have to be more careful from here on," Nikki said. "But don't worry, guys. There's no way I'm gonna let this old fire get the best of us."

CHAPTER 6

Nikki led her charges down a forest trail away from the fire. "Listen." She searched the tops of the trees. As she did, she stumbled over a tree root and nearly fell. Molly clung to her neck, choking her.

It was getting close to dusk. She put the curly-headed little girl down under a tree, shaded her eyes, and scanned the patches of hazy sky.

The sound drew closer. It was a sort of vibration.

A helicopter.

It came in fast. The rotors whipped and beat the air in a heavy pulse. It was so loud she knew it had to be flying low. Possibly it was a search and rescue team looking for them.

Nikki waved and yelled, hoping to attract the pilot's attention. She grabbed the walkie-talkie from James's hand. "Emergency, repeat, this is an emergency—can you copy?"

The helicopter closed quickly and sounded as if it were coming straight at them. For less than a second she caught a glimpse of its bright navigation lights as it passed directly overhead. Then it disappeared.

Nikki continued to wave and call out, hoping the chopper would circle back and see her. She stared at the gap in the trees, wanting desperately to see the helicopter return. But she knew it wouldn't come back. It was gone.

"Why din't he stop for us?" A big tear rolled down Molly's cheek and plopped on her checked shirt.

Nikki sat under the big tree beside her. "It wasn't his fault, Molly. He just couldn't see us." She took the little girl's hand. "But I don't want you to worry. We're going to be safe."

James knelt beside them. "But we're way up in these mountains. How are we ever going to find our way out?"

"Hey, didn't I tell you not to worry? It may take a while, but I promise—I'll get you out of this."

Molly sniffled and made an attempt to wipe her nose. "I'm hungry."

"I can fix that." Nikki rummaged through her backpack and came up with some trail mix and elk jerky. "Try some of Nikki's special homemade jerky. Actually it's my dad's recipe, but I made it."

While the children ate, Nikki rolled her shoulders and stretched. She hadn't realized until now how tired she was. Molly was small, but after a couple of miles of being carried up and down these hills, she got heavy.

"I'm sleepy." Molly rubbed her eyes with a dirty hand.

"I know you are, but we can't stop here. We have to get as far from the fire as possible before dark."

She handed the toy walkie-talkie back to

James. "Is this what you used to call for help earlier?"

James nodded. "I brought it with us when we left on our trip this morning. I think it's broke now."

"Your trip?"

"Me and Molly got up early before anybody else and took a trip in Grandpa's canoe. We were only going to be gone for a little while. But the river dragged us for miles and miles, and then we crashed on some rocks—"

"It was scary," Molly interrupted. "We almost din't make it out of the water."

"We walked for a real long time," James continued. "Then we saw the fire and started running. That's when Molly fell down on that ledge."

Nikki thought about how lucky the children were. About how Molly could have fallen all the way to the bottom of Deadman's Drop or how they might have been caught on that ledge in a raging inferno. She touched the little girl's ankle. "The swelling seems to be going down. It doesn't look broken. Just badly bruised and maybe sprained."

Even though they were well away from the fire, Nikki was still concerned. The air smelled of smoke, and the wind could change direction at any minute and catch them off guard.

She stood and lifted Molly up in her arms. "We'd better get going. We'll make camp later, when I'm positive we're out of danger."

CHAPTER 7

 When it was too dark to see any longer, Nikki pulled a flashlight from her bag, laid Molly down, and covered her up to her chin with dry leaves and grass. The little girl had gone to sleep while hanging on Nikki's back.

It seemed ridiculous to make a fire after what they had just been through, but Nikki knew it had to be done. Temperatures in the mountains dropped suddenly at night, and they had no coats or blankets.

While James collected wood, Nikki cleared a spot for the fire and dug a small hole with her hands. Using pine needles for tinder and matches from her pack, she quickly had a blaze going.

"Move those rocks James and make yourself a bed—like I did for Molly. You'll sleep snug as a bug."

A high-pitched scream ripped through the night.

James jumped. He shivered and moved closer to Nikki. "What was that?"

"I'd say it was a mountain lion." Nikki tossed a rock out of her way, sat down, and pulled dry leaves over her feet. "They sound a lot like people sometimes."

"Do they eat you?"

For the first time Nikki noticed just how scared the boy was. Still, he was trying his best to be brave. She reached over and tousled his hair. "I said I wouldn't let anything happen to you, didn't I? Try to get some sleep. We've got a lot of walking to do tomorrow."

James sat back down. "Do you know where we are?"

Nikki hesitated. "Not exactly. I haven't ever been to this part of the mountains before, but I do have a general idea how far away from my house we are. I figure if we start out early in the morning, we should be home by nightfall. Then we'll call your grandparents and let them know where you are."

"My dad's gonna be awful mad at me. He and my mom were coming to pick us up to-day."

Nikki shrugged. "Who knows? Maybe he'll just be glad you're safe."

James shook his head. "He told me to take extra good care of Molly while they were gone and not let anything happen to her."

"Then he can't be too mad." Nikki looked at the sleeping little girl. Her chubby cheeks were shiny and pink in the firelight. "I'd say Molly's doing just fine."

James lay back on the ground. "Nikki?"

"Yes?"

"I'm glad you came to help us."

CHAPTER 8

Bright sunlight woke Nikki from a restless sleep. By the position of the sun she could tell that she had slept later than she wanted to. It was midmorning. She rose quickly and poured dirt on the campfire until it was completely out. Then she shook James and Molly awake.

The exhausted group started across the mountain in the direction of the lodge. The trail was rugged. Thick tree roots and fallen branches made every step treacherous. After several hours Nikki pulled the children up a steep rise and called for a rest.

From the top of the high mountain peak they looked down on the blackened forest, still smoking in places. In the center of this once solid green paradise was now a hideously charred scar that stretched for miles. The fire had destroyed the entire face of one hillside and a valley and had then burned itself out at the river.

Nikki knew enough about the mountains and fire not to trust appearances. All it would take was a strong wind, and those smoldering embers could be whipped into another huge blaze.

"Break's over." Nikki stood. Her back and the calves of her legs were beginning to ache. They hurt when she reached down to pick up Molly. "Come on, Little Red Riding Hood, let's hurry up and get through these woods."

Molly giggled. "Are we going to Grandma's house?"

Nikki shook her head. "Nope. We're going to my house. There's no big bad wolf there."

James got to his feet and picked up the

backpack. "How much longer till we get there? Seems like we've been walking forever."

Nikki thought about it. If they continued to cut straight across the mountain, they could be there in a couple more hours. On the other hand, that way would take them dangerously close to the edge of the burn. She studied their faces. They were so tired. Nikki didn't know how much longer they could hold out.

Before she could make the decision, they heard the sound of a small engine. Nikki's face brightened. Firefighters.

"Come on, guys, maybe they can help us."

They ran toward the noise, slipping and weaving through the trees. At the bottom of the hill was a small clearing completely surrounded by forest and hidden from the fire and the world. Tents were set up, and two men were standing in front of them, talking.

"Hello!" Nikki shouted, and waved from the fringe of the trees.

The man with his back to them turned. Nikki stopped in her tracks. It was Red Beard, the poacher. She glanced around the camp. There were rifles leaning against a tree and a beautiful ram's head lying on a piece of plastic on the ground. Two camouflage-colored four-wheelers were parked near the tents.

Nikki swallowed and kept walking. She tried to act as if nothing were wrong. "Excuse me, sir. We're lost, and we were just wondering if—"

Red Beard strode over to them. "What are you doing here?"

Molly peeked over Nikki's shoulder. "We crashed in the water and nearly got burned up. Then Nikki found us, and now we're going to her house to be safe."

The man's piercing blue eyes glowered at the little girl. "And just where exactly is Nikki's house?"

Molly hid her face in Nikki's shoulder. "We're not sure exactly." Nikki moved Molly around to the front and held her close. "Like I said, we're lost."

James touched the curled horn on the ram's head. "Are you guys hunters?"

The other man, the one Nikki remembered as Frank, moved in behind them. He picked up one of the rifles and stood with his feet apart, pointing it threateningly. "Get inside that tent. All of you—now!"

Nikki held Molly with one arm and took James's hand. "Come on, kids. Do what the man says."

There was barely room for all of them to sit down inside the tent. Nikki put Molly on the sleeping bag. Her mind raced. What had she gotten them into? All along she had promised to take care of them, and then, like an idiot, she'd walked right into danger.

She rubbed her forehead and tried to think. These were cruel men—criminals. They had guns and probably wouldn't hesitate to use them.

Molly pulled on her sleeve. "Those men are bad."

"Yes, they are. Very bad."

"What are we going to do, Nikki?" James asked worriedly.

She didn't have an answer for him. They could hear the two men arguing outside the tent. Frank was angry. "I say we get rid of them now, Strecker. No one will know. They'll think the fire got 'em."

"We'll wait. People are probably looking for those kids."

Frank snarled. "All the more reason to take what we have and get out of here before they find us."

"Maybe you're right." Strecker moved away, and they had to strain to hear his voice. "We'll pack everything and leave in the morning."

"What about the kids?"

"We'll take care of them early, before we go."

The tent flap flung open, causing Nikki to fall back with a start. Frank jerked the sleeping bag out from under Molly.

"Sweet dreams, kids." He sneered evilly at them.

"What are they gonna do to us?" James whispered when Frank had gone.

"Nothing." Nikki bit her lip. She felt in her pocket for her knife. "They're not going to get the chance. You and Molly try to get some sleep now. When I wake you, don't ask questions. Just be ready to go."

CHAPTER 9

 Frank had laid the sleeping bag just outside the tent's opening. His sleeping body blocked any escape through the door.

Nikki could hear him snoring. James and Molly were huddled in one corner, using each other for pillows. She pulled out her pocketknife and scooted to the back wall of the tent. Quietly she slit the canvas all the way down, then stepped out and moved around to the front. The moon gave her enough light to see where she was going.

To the four-wheelers.

They were so sure of themselves the men hadn't thought to remove the keys. She unfolded her knife and punctured the tires of one of the vehicles. Then she threw that set of keys into the woods.

Frank made a choking, sputtering noise and sat up. Nikki crouched behind one of the four-wheelers. The big man looked around a moment and then lay back down facing her. In the darkness she couldn't tell if his eyes were open or closed.

She waited for what seemed like hours until she heard his even snoring.

Then she moved to the guns.

One was a high-powered rifle with a bolt. Her dad had one just like it, and she'd seen him use it many times. She slid the bolt out and put it in her pocket. The other gun had a lever action. Nikki felt on the ground for rocks the size of the barrel. With a stick she forced three of them down into it.

Time was running out. Nikki made her way back to the slit in the tent and gently awakened James. "Time to go."

James didn't say a word. He helped her pick up Molly, grabbed the pack, and followed her out of the tent.

They sat Molly on the seat of the four-wheeler, put it in neutral, and pushed it down the valley. They hadn't gone far when Nikki heard yelling. The men were awake and had obviously discovered the empty tent.

"Get on, James!" Nikki put Molly on her lap, turned the key, and pushed the start button.

Nothing.

It wouldn't start. "Come on . . ." She pushed the button again. The machine made a grinding noise and then slowly worked its way into motion.

Nikki kicked it in gear, found the headlight switch, and roared into the forest. She had to pick her way carefully. Even though she had driven her uncle Joe's four-wheeler many times, there wasn't much room to maneuver, and she didn't want to make any mistakes.

Behind them they heard the two men bellowing and cursing over the other disabled four-wheeler. Nikki smiled. Wait until they checked out their guns.

On through the dark night she drove without stopping. After a while James tapped her on the shoulder. "How can you tell which way we're going?"

She pointed at the sky. "Up there. See the Big Dipper?"

"I think so."

"Line up the two stars at the top of the dipper. See that shiny star off to the right? That's called the North Star. You can find your way around at night if you know which direction to travel. Right now we're heading south. And if I don't wreck us, we should run into my house in about a half hour."

CHAPTER 10

 The four-wheeler trembled. Then it sputtered and jerked to a complete stop.

Nikki sighed. "Well, that's it. We must be out of gas. Looks like we walk from here."

James was too tired to say anything. He just climbed off and fell in step beside her.

Nikki was stiff from carrying Molly. She shook out her arms one at a time. Awake Molly was heavy, but asleep she was like a lead weight. Every muscle in Nikki's body screamed at her to stop and rest.

She held the flashlight in the crook of her

arm and kept walking. All the trees and land-marks looked alike in the dark. Undoubtedly they were moving in the right direction, but that didn't guarantee they were heading straight for the lodge. Unless she saw some-thing familiar soon, they would have to turn around and search behind them.

The moon had gone behind some clouds, and it was difficult to see where they were going. Forty-five minutes or more had passed, and Nikki was sure she had somehow missed the lodge in the darkness. It was possible that she had walked right past the house without even knowing it.

Then she heard it. A horse's whinny.

Goblin.

She moved to the sound and in a few yards nearly ran smack into the back of the corrals. Somehow she had managed to lead them to the far side of the lodge. If it hadn't been for Goblin, she might have kept going until day-light.

Nikki headed for the house. She stopped on the front porch. It felt so good to be home.

"We're here."

James was half asleep behind her. His eyes fluttered open. "Is this it? Is this your house?"

"Home sweet home." She hefted Molly onto her hip and led the way into the house. Upstairs Nikki tucked Molly and James into her bed. They were asleep before their heads hit the pillows. Nikki moved for the telephone.

There was still no dial tone, only the soft whisper of static.

The chances of someone's listening to the CB at this time of night were small, but for the children's sake, she plodded into her dad's office and picked up the handset. "If anyone can hear me, we have an emergency at Tall Pines Hunting Lodge. Repeat, this is an emergency."

Nikki called for help until she fell asleep on the desk still holding the receiver.

The big grandfather clock in the hall struck six. Nikki's head jerked to attention. She couldn't believe it. She had actually fallen asleep at the controls.

She tried calling out again. There was still

no response. It was useless. Whatever she was going to do, it would have to be on her own.

Through the window she noticed the horses milling around the water tank. They hadn't been fed the entire time she was gone. "Boy, I'm a fine one to leave in charge." Nikki headed outside to look after them.

Goblin seemed glad to see her. He nuzzled her with his soft white nose. Nikki patted him. "I wish you could help me, boy. Got any suggestions on how to get these kids home? Maybe we'll all pile on you and take off upriver. What do you say?"

"I'd like that."

Nikki turned. James was standing behind her. She smiled. "I didn't expect you to be up yet."

"That clock woke me up."

"Me too." She broke up some hay and threw it into the feeding trough. "Do you ride, James?"

The boy looked down. "No." He glanced up at her. "I sure would like to try, though."

Nikki ran her hand through her hair. "We have a problem, James. The telephone's dead, and I can't pick up anyone on the CB. You and Molly may have to stay with me until Sunday, when my parents get home."

James made a face. "My dad will be worried sick."

"I know. I've been racking my brain, trying to figure out how to get you home."

"Can't you just drive us?"

Nikki was flattered that he thought she was old enough to drive but didn't say so. Instead she told him that her parents had taken the only vehicle except for a broken-down jeep in the barn.

"What about the horses?" James's face was hopeful.

"I thought about that. But the only cabins I can remember anywhere upriver are near Waterton. Is that where your grandfather lives?"

The boy nodded. "We go there every summer for vacation."

Nikki frowned. "Waterton is over sixty miles away, James. By the time we got there my parents would have been back and could have driven you."

"Maybe we could carry gas to the four-wheeler and use it to go home on."

Nikki hadn't thought of that. It was a possibility. The poachers had probably cleared out of the woods by now, worried that their escaped captives had made it to a phone and called the sheriff.

"That's not a bad idea, James. After breakfast we may just give it a try."

CHAPTER 11

Molly bit into a piece of toast. "You're a real good cooker, Nikki."

Nikki laughed. "Yeah, it takes a special talent to pour milk on a bowl of Crunchy Smacks."

"Are we going to take gas to the four-wheeler now?" James asked.

"You finish your breakfast. I'll fill the gas can and go after the four-wheeler. It may take me a while to find it. You and Molly can watch TV until I get back."

James's lower lip went out. "I'd rather go with you."

"I know you would, but Molly needs the rest. Okay?"

He looked at his feet. "Okay."

Nikki patted him on the back. "I knew I could count on you." She squeezed Molly and started out the door. "I'll be back as soon as I find it."

The last thing she wanted to do was take another hike into the woods. But she remembered how good it felt when she finally made it home last night. James and Molly needed to get to their home, too.

The gas can was on a shelf in the boat shed. Luckily it was three-quarters full. She grabbed it and was on her way out when she heard voices.

Through a crack in the door she saw someone in the yard. She pushed the door open a little wider.

It was Frank, and he was carrying one of the rifles.

Nikki drew a sharp breath. She watched him walk around the house, looking in the windows. In a few minutes he was joined at the side of the house by Strecker.

She couldn't make out their words. But she could hear them laugh and saw them move to the porch.

It was easy for them. Frank turned the knob on the front door, and they walked right in. Nikki sank to the floor and closed her eyes. Why hadn't she prepared for this? Anyone with half a brain would have at least considered the possibility that the poachers might find them. Now, because of her stupidity, the kids were alone in the house with criminals.

She tried to gather her thoughts. It was her fault the kids were in this mess, and she would just have to get them out.

She pushed the shed door open barely wide enough to squeeze through. Keeping low, she ran to the barn. Goblin saw her and trotted up.

"I'm gonna need your help, old boy." Nikki slipped a bridle over his ears and saddled him. She led him out the back door into the forest.

Staying in the trees, she circled the lodge and came in behind it. She tied Goblin securely to a branch and moved to the tree line at the edge of the forest.

She watched the house. There was no movement. Nikki took a deep breath. Somehow she had to make it from the trees to the back of the house without being seen. The only way was to run for it.

Nikki hunched over and ran for all she was worth. When she reached the house, her heart was racing—not because she was tired but because she was afraid the poachers might have seen her.

She waited.

No one came out.

Staying close to the wall, she made her way to the bathroom window. It was the only one she knew for certain wouldn't be locked.

As quietly as possible, she slid the window open and pulled herself up and over the windowsill. Again she waited, but no one came.

Nikki swallowed and opened the bathroom door an inch at a time.

Frank and Strecker were in the den. Nikki could hear them talking over the noise of the television. Apparently they were waiting for her to come back. The kids must have told them where she was going.

The carpet muffled the noise as she crawled down the hall on her hands and knees. At the door to the den she sat on her heels and leaned back against the wall. If the criminals saw her, it was all over.

She took another deep breath and peeked around the corner. Luckily the poachers had their backs to her. Molly was watching cartoons, and James was sitting on the sofa, staring at the ceiling.

Nikki waved at him. The first couple of times he didn't see her. The third time his face lit up. He sat up straight and stared at her. She ducked behind the wall.

Frank growled at the boy. "What are you lookin' at, kid?"

James slumped back on the couch. "Nothing." He sat up again. "Mister?"

"What do you want?"

"My sister needs to go to the bathroom."

Molly turned around and looked up at her brother. She was about to protest, but the calm expression on James's face kept her quiet.

Frank's eyes narrowed. "She looks fine to me, kid. Sit down and shut up."

"Okay. But don't say I didn't warn you."

"Let him take the girl to the john," Strecker snapped. "They're not going anywhere."

James took Molly by the hand and started to lead her out of the room. Frank grabbed his arm. "You come right back, squirt, 'cause if I have to come lookin' for you . . ." He drew his finger across the boy's throat. "Got the picture?"

James nodded and moved to the door. Nikki was waiting down the hall in the bathroom. She motioned for them to hurry.

When Molly saw her, she smiled and started to talk. Nikki put her finger to her lips and pulled her inside the room.

She pointed to the window and gave James a leg up. When he was safely out, Nikki handed Molly to him and slid out behind them.

"This way," Nikki whispered. She led them to the tree where Goblin was waiting. "I know you guys don't ride, so listen to me. All I want you to do is hold on tight. Got it?"

"We got it." James helped her lift Molly onto the swells of the saddle. Nikki quickly untied the rope from the branch, climbed into the seat, and pulled James on behind.

"Where are we going?" James asked.

Nikki urged Goblin through the trees. "I don't know. All I know is we have to get away from here."

"There they are!" Frank was pointing and yelling from the bathroom window.

"Hang on." James wrapped his arms around her waist as Nikki moved Goblin into a trot. She held Molly in her lap to keep the little girl from falling while she guided the horse with her free hand.

Chapter 12

Goblin took a long drink of cool river water. Nikki splashed some on her face and then took a drink herself.

James and Molly were playing near the shore. Nikki looked behind her. She didn't hear anything, but this time she wasn't going to take any chances.

Goblin was covered with a white lather. They had ridden him hard and covered several miles. He needed a rest. She decided to let Molly ride while she and James walked for a while.

"Come on, guys. Time to get going." Nikki

lifted the little girl into the saddle. "Hold on tight to the saddle horn, Molly."

James hadn't said a word since they left the lodge, and Nikki was worried about him. "Are you okay, partner?"

He looked up at her. "Do you think they'll find us?"

"Not if I can help it."

"That big man said he was going to use a knife on me if we ran away."

Nikki rested her arm on his shoulders. "You know, James, it just occurred to me that I haven't told you what a big help you've been during all this. I couldn't have done any of it without you."

"Really?"

"Yeah. I don't think those poachers have a chance against us. Together we're too smart for them."

James beamed. "Do you have a plan?"

"Sure," Nikki lied. "There are bound to be people downriver somewhere, making sure that fire is under control. We'll just ask one of them to help us out."

James seemed satisfied with her answer. Nikki wished she were. In an area that big, the chances of running into someone were remote at best.

Goblin stopped walking. Nikki pulled on the reins. He stumbled a few steps, favoring his right front leg, and then stopped again.

Nikki picked up the leg and looked at the underside. The soft frog of the horse's foot had a large thorn in it. She lifted Molly to the ground and jerked the thorn out. Blood squirted from the hole.

There was nothing she could do for him. If they kept riding him, he might become permanently injured. Nikki pulled his saddle and bridle off and put them under a tree.

"You know the way home, fella. When you feel like it, you head on back there." Nikki ran her hand down his neck. She turned and picked up Molly. "I guess you'll have to put up with me now. Goblin can't carry you anymore."

Nikki had just settled Molly on her own

back when they heard something crashing through the brush behind them. She grabbed James's sleeve and pulled him down behind some bushes.

Two of her father's horses galloped by—ridden by Frank and Strecker.

James's face was white. They were going to get caught, and he knew it.

Nikki stood up cautiously. "They'll be back when they lose our trail. We have to stay in the brush and hope they miss us." She looked down the shore. Things here seemed familiar.

Of course. She'd been here two days ago when she had come to rescue the kids. She knelt back down. "James, if it isn't burned up, I have a canoe somewhere nearby. Molly, don't make a sound. We're going to work our way down the shore, and we don't want those bad men to find us."

Walking slowly and staying in the bushes, they moved along the riverbank. They were getting close to the burn, and Nikki was afraid they had missed the canoe.

"There's something." James pointed to some brush ahead of them.

It was the canoe. The fire hadn't damaged it.

Nikki handed Molly to James, ran to untie the slipknot from around the tree, and moved the canoe into the water. "Hurry, kids. Get in."

She slipped Molly's arms into the life vest and reached out to push off.

"I wouldn't do that." Frank's voice boomed from above her.

Nikki looked up—into the barrel of his rifle.

"You've given us enough problems. Step out of that canoe."

Nikki closed her eyes.

And pushed.

The canoe floated a few feet out into the water.

Frank aimed the gun at the canoe and pulled the trigger. There was a moment's hesitation, followed by a deafening explosion.

Nikki looked back. It was awful. Frank lay on the ground covered with blood. She'd never intended for anything like this to happen. Her only thought had been to stop the poachers from hurting the kids.

Strecker ran along the shore after them, screaming threats as he clawed through the heavy brush.

Nikki kept paddling.

CHAPTER 13

Everything they passed on one side of the river was charred and black. On the other side was a vertical rock slab that separated the river's two forks.

Nikki concentrated on her new problem. Deadman's Drop was ahead of them somewhere. The current was swifter now, and it was all she could do to keep the canoe from turning on her.

She needed to get back to shore. But the river had a mind of its own. Every time she got close, the current snatched them and drove them farther out into a crashing torrent.

They couldn't hear anything above the roar of the falls. The shore drew nearer but not fast enough. They smashed into something beneath the water. There was a ripping sound. Nikki looked down and saw a sharp piece of rock tearing through the fiberglass bottom.

The canoe stopped momentarily, then lurched. Water sprayed through the floor, filling the hull. It shot forward and rammed another set of rocks.

Nikki's arms ached. She could hardly move the paddles. The river was winning. It seemed ready to swallow them up.

James yelled at her. She couldn't make his words out above the noise of the rapids. He pointed wildly to shore.

She turned. Forest rangers and firefighters were standing on the bank. They had a long rope and were trying to throw it out to them. Every time they threw, they missed.

The canoe grated on the rocks. Nikki knew it wouldn't stay snagged long.

It started moving again. The current had dislodged it, and the canoe was coming around. The ranger onshore coiled the rope and threw it out.

It was now or never. Nikki lunged for the rope, caught it, and fell into the water. The force of the river drove her into the rocks and pinned her there.

James held a paddle out to her. She wrapped the rope around one arm and reached for the oar. Her fingertips had barely touched it when the river slammed her back against the rocks and down under the water. Her mind carried one thought.

Air.

She broke the surface and took in great gulps. Another rapid washed over her. Everything went dark as the churning water tossed her body about like a rag doll. Just when she thought her lungs would burst, a swell swept Nikki back up.

The little canoe was quickly filling with water. James valiantly held the paddle out to her again. Nikki pushed her exhausted legs against the rocks and stretched as far as possible.

And made it.

Once she had a grip on the paddle, she used it to draw the craft closer to her. When she finally had her hand on the side of the canoe, the men on the bank started pulling them in, heaving until they dragged it into the shallows.

Nikki crawled to shore and fell on the bank.

Voices echoed.

". . . the little boy said something about poachers and a gun blowing up . . . we've radioed the sheriff's chopper to pick them up . . . miracle they're still alive . . . find the parents . . ."

The voices sounded hollow and unreal, mixed with the roar of the rapids.

Nikki's eyes opened. The men had wrapped them in blankets. James was sitting on the bank, and Molly was perched on a ranger's lap, listening to his assurances that the sheriff would have the "mean men" in custody soon.

"Are you all right?" One of the rangers handed Nikki a cup of cocoa.

Nikki managed a weak smile and took a long sip. They were better than all right.

They were safe.

GARY PAULSEN
ADVENTURE GUIDE

FOREST FIRE SURVIVAL

During hot, dry periods forest fires are a threat to hikers and wilderness users. There are several basic rules to follow if you should get caught in one.

A fire must have oxygen in order to burn. The amount of wind will determine how fast and how far the fire will spread. Pay attention to the wind direction, and don't run downwind from a fire. It is best to move at a right angle to the wind.

Try to head downhill from a fire. Fire naturally spreads faster uphill than down. Do not climb steep hills or canyons on which you may get trapped.

Remain calm, and try to think rationally. If possible, find water, a moist area, or a bare spot that will not burn easily.

Avoid inhaling smoke by staying low with your face down on the ground. To protect your lungs, breathe through a damp cloth or your shirt.

To help prevent forest fires, make sure campfires are out completely before leaving a campsite. Protect flammable materials from wind, and be sure to properly discard litter that may spread a fire.

Don't miss all the exciting action!

**Read the other action-packed books
in Gary Paulsen's
WORLD OF ADVENTURE!**

The Legend of Red Horse Cavern

William Little Bear Tucker and his friend Sarah
Thompson have heard the eerie Apache legend many
times. Will's grandfather especially loves to tell them
about Red Horse—an Indian brave who betrayed his
people, was beheaded, and now haunts the Sacra-
mento Mountain range, searching for his head. To Will
and Sarah it's just a story—until they decide to explore
a newfound mountain cave, a cave filled with dangerous treasures.

Deep underground Will and Sarah uncover an old
chest stuffed with a million dollars. But now armed
bandits are after them. When they find a gold Apache
statue hidden in a skull, it seems Red Horse is hunting
them, too. Then they lose their way, and each step they
take in the damp dark cavern could be their last.

Rodomonte's Revenge

Friends Brett Wilder and Tom Houston are video game
whizzes. So when a new virtual reality arcade called
Rodomonte's Revenge opens near their home, they
make sure they're its first customers. The game is awe-
some. There are flaming fire rivers to jump, beastly
buzz-bugs to fight, and ugly tunnel spiders to escape. If
they're good enough they'll face Rodomonte, an evil
giant waiting to do battle within his hidden castle.

But soon after they play the game, strange things start happening to Brett and Tom. The computer is taking over their minds. Now everything that happens in the game is happening in real life. A buzz-bug could gnaw off their ears. Rodomonte could smash them to bits. Brett and Tom have no choice but to play Rodomonte's Revenge again. This time they'll be playing for their lives.

Look for these adventures coming soon!

The Rock Jockeys

Devil's Wall.

Rick Williams and his friends J.D. and Spud—the Rock Jockeys—are attempting to become the first and youngest climbers to ascend the north face of their area's most treacherous mountain. They're also out to discover if a B-17 bomber rumored to have crashed into the mountain years ago is really there.

As the Rock Jockeys explore Devil's Wall, they stumble upon the plane's battered shell. Inside, they find items that seem to have belonged to the crew, including a diary written by the navigator. Spud later falls into a deep hole and finds something even more frightening: a human skull and bones. To find out where they might have come from, the boys read the navigator's story in the diary. It reveals a gruesome secret that heightens the dangers the mountain might hold for the Rock Jockeys.

Hook 'Em, Snotty!

Bobbie Walker loves working on her grandfather's ranch. She hates the fact that her cousin Alex is coming up from Los Angeles to visit and will probably ruin her summer. Alex can barely ride a horse and doesn't know the first thing about roping. There is no way Alex can survive a ride into the flats to round up wild cattle. But Bobbie is going to have to let her tag along anyway.

Out in the flats the weather turns bad. Even worse, Bobbie knows that she'll have to watch out for the Bledsoe boys, two mischievous brothers who are usually up to no good. When the boys rustle the girls' cattle, Bobbie and Alex team up to teach the Bledsoes a lesson. But with the wild bull Diablo on the loose, the fun and games may soon turn deadly serious.

Danger on Midnight River

Daniel Martin doesn't want to go to Camp Eagle Nest. He wants to spend the summer as he always does: with his uncle Smitty in the Rocky Mountains. Daniel is a slow learner, but most other kids call him retarded. Daniel knows that at camp, things are only going to get worse. His nightmare comes true when he and three bullies must ride the camp van together.

On the trip to camp Daniel is the butt of the bullies' jokes. He ignores them and concentrates on the roads outside. He thinks they may be lost. As the van crosses a wooden bridge, the planks suddenly give way. The van plunges into the raging river below. Daniel struggles to shore, but the driver and the other boys are nowhere to be found. It's freezing, and night is setting in. Daniel faces a difficult decision. He could save himself . . . or risk everything to try to rescue the others, too.

The Gorgon Slayer

Eleven-year-old Warren Trumbull has a strange job. He works for Prince Charming's Damsel in Distress Rescue Agency, saving people from hideous monsters, evil warlocks, and wicked witches. Then one day Warren gets the most dangerous assignment of all: He must exterminate a Gorgon.

Gorgons are horrible creatures. They have green scales, clawed fingers, and snakes for hair. They also have the power to turn people to stone. Warren doesn't want to be a stone statue for the rest of his life. He'll need all his courage and skill—and his secret plan—to become a true Gorgon slayer.

The Gorgon howls as Warren enters the dark basement to do battle. Warren lowers his eyes, raises his sword and shield, and leaps into action. But will his plan work?

GARY PAULSEN
WORLD OF ADVENTURE

CHART YOUR COURSE TO EXCITEMENT!

Take the journey of a lifetime with *Gary Paulsen World of Adventure!* Every story is a thrilling, action-packed odyssey, containing an adventure guide with important survival tips no camper or adventurer should be without!

Order any or all of these exciting **Gary Paulsen** adventures. Just check off the titles you want, then fill out and mail the order form below.

☐	0-440-41023-1	**LEGEND OF RED HORSE CAVERN**	$3.50/$4.50 Can.
☐	0-440-41024-X	**RODOMONTE'S REVENGE**	$3.50/$4.50 Can.
☐	0-440-41025-8	**ESCAPE FROM FIRE MOUNTAIN**	$3.50/$4.50 Can.
☐	0-440-41026-6	**THE ROCK JOCKEYS**	$3.50/$4.50 Can.

Bantam Doubleday Dell
Books For Young Readers

BDD BOOKS FOR YOUNG READERS
2451 South Wolf Road
Des Plaines, IL 60018

Please send me the items I have checked above. I am enclosing $_____
(please add $2.50 to cover postage and handling).
Send check or money order, no cash or C.O.D.s please.

NAME _____

ADDRESS _____

CITY _____ STATE _____ ZIP _____

Please allow four to six weeks for delivery.
Prices and availability subject to change without notice.   BFYR 115 3/95

CULPEPPER ADVENTURES

For laugh-out-loud fun, join Dunc and Amos and take the Culpepper challenge!
Gary Paulsen's Culpepper Adventures—
Bet you can't read just one!

☐ 0-440-40790-7 DUNC AND AMOS AND THE RED TATTOOS.....$3.25/$3.99 Can.
☐ 0-440-40874-1 DUNC'S UNDERCOVER CHRISTMAS...............$3.50/$4.50 Can.
☐ 0-440-40883-0 THE WILD CULPEPPER CRUISE.......................$3.50/$4.50 Can.
☐ 0-440-40893-8 DUNC AND THE HAUNTED CASTLE.................$3.50/$4.50 Can.
☐ 0-440-40902-0 COWPOKES AND DESPERADOES....................$3.50/$4.50 Can.
☐ 0-440-40928-4 PRINCE AMOS..$3.50/$4.50 Can.
☐ 0-440-40930-6 COACH AMOS..$3.50/$4.50 Can.
☐ 0-440-40990-X AMOS AND THE ALIENS...................................$3.50/$4.50 Can.

Bantam Doubleday Dell
Books for Young Readers

Bantam Doubleday Dell Books for Young Readers
2451 South Wolf Road
Des Plaines, IL 60018

Please send the items I have checked above. I'm enclosing $_____ (please add $2.50 to cover postage and handling). Send check or money order, no cash or C.O.D.s please.

Name _____

Address _____

City _____ State _____ Zip _____

Please allow four to six weeks for delivery.
Prices and availability subject to change without notice.   **BFYR 29 6/94**

Thrilling Novels from Three-Time Newbery Honor Book Author
GARY PAULSEN

Did you ever wish you could build a raft and travel down a treacherous river? Did you ever wonder what it was like to live during World War II? Or did you ever think it would be great to travel to places you've never been before? Now you can. Gary Paulsen, three-time Newbery Honor Book author, takes you on more wondrous journeys filled with laughs, discovery and adventure.

☐ 40782-6	**THE MONUMENT**	$3.99/$4.99 Can.
☐ 40753-2	**THE RIVER**	$3.99/$4.99 Can.
☐ 40364-2	**VOYAGE OF THE *FROG***	$3.50/$4.25 Can.
☐ 40524-6	**THE BOY WHO OWNED THE SCHOOL**	$3.50/$4.25 Can.
☐ 40454-1	**THE WINTER ROOM**	$3.50/$4.25 Can.
☐ 40704-4	**THE COOKCAMP**	$3.50/$4.50 Can.

Bantam Doubleday Dell
Books For Young Readers

Buy them at your local bookstore or use this handy page for ordering.

BDD BOOKS FOR YOUNG READERS
2451 S. Wolf Road
Des Plaines, IL 60018

Please send me the items I have checked above. I am enclosing $_____ (please add $2.50 to cover postage and handling). Send check or money order, no cash or C.O.D.s please.

MR./MS. _____

ADDRESS _____

CITY _____ STATE _____ ZIP _____